David Rix is an author, composer, editor, artist and publisher active in the area of Slipstream, Speculative Fiction and Horror. Idée fixes include our natural identities, contemporary classical music, the seashore, urban underground, railways, rocks and canals. His published books are *What the Giants were Saying,* the novelette *A Suite in Four Windows,* and the novella/story collection *Feather*, which was shortlisted for the Edge Hill prize. In addition, his works have appeared in various places, the most notable being many of the *Strange Tales* series of anthologies from Tartarus Press, *Monster Book For Girls* from Exaggerated Press, *Creeping Crawlers* from Shadow Publishing, and *Marked to Die* from Snuggly Books. He also runs and creates the art for Eibonvale Press, which focuses on innovative and unusual new slipstream writing. As an editor, his first anthology *Rustblind and Silverbright*, a collection of Slipstream stories connected to the railways, was shortlisted for the British Fantasy Award in the Best Anthology category. He is currently at work on two first novels, any one of which might win the race – *A Blast of Hunters* and *Stink Horn.*

Brown is the New Black
(A Prelude After the Breakdown)

theEXAGGERATEDpress UK
http://exaggeratedpress.weebly.com/

Brown is the New Black
(A Prelude After the Breakdown)

David Rix

Published by theEXAGGERATEDpress UK
http://exaggeratedpress.weebly.com/

The sound of gunfire was always an alien thing in London. Even now, in the silence. Maybe there were places where it was less so – where it had been more mundane. Places where flickers of war, violence, machismo or delusion still distorted reality. But not London. That was why the skin still prickled at the distant sound – why it made Jess and Jay dart into a shadowy corner, dropping the two heavily loaded black rucksacks they were carrying and crouching into a knot.

They were both dressed in black from mask to boots – and this was why. Camouflage.

"Gawd sake," Jess muttered under her breath, "you can't even nip to the shops anymore . . ."

Barely any lights pierced the darkness – the ghostly dark world of London where no street lamps shone, no windows glowed – but paradoxically that made it less dark rather than more, at least when the moon was out. Easier to see rather than harder. That was one of the many surprises since the world had changed. And now they held on to each other tightly, preserving the frozen stillness but also finding comfort. The feel of warm life – someone else's heart racing in tense caution – the almost imperceptible sounds of two black-clad bodies trying not to move . . .

In the middle distance, a figure came into view, looking round cautiously. There was something in his hand. Something small and gleaming and alien . . .

A hunter. Jess swore – the quietest swearword he had ever heard in his life, barely even any breath to it but still perfectly audible to him, conveyed through feel as much as sound.

And he was looking at them. The gun held in a position of caution, not aggression. What this gun was intended for did not tend to crouch hidden in the shadows.

"Who are you?" he called at last, his familiar British accent again coming with a touch of the surreal in such circumstances. "I can see you. So just tell me who you are."

7

Without a word, the two unknotted themselves and bolted down the street, leaving the rucksacks behind.

"Wait," the hunter called. "Oh for fuck's sake . . ."

They ran. He was aware of her moving beside him like a black ghost – like a hole in the night. They dashed between the parked cars and into a side street, then round several corners of what had once been drab London housing estate. It seemed deserted now. No hunters or hunted. In the middle of it all was a small green area – one of the innumerable tiny parks that filled the city, just trees and *Keep of the grass* signs, with a few token efforts at ornamentation. The sort of place where the kids would have congregated or where hassled workers might have grabbed a few minutes' peace sitting in the shade. Once upon a time. Now there were only moths, drifting past as small pale blurs – like ghosts in the air.

They slipped into the bushes, separately this time, and froze again, listening for any sound of following feet. But there was nothing. The city might have been empty. Only the moths moved – and the silence was so deep that when one came close, he could hear it clearly – a whirring noise like a cat's purr.

He realised that he could still see her, crouched in the middle distance – an area of dark that was somehow different. That shouldn't be right. This was an outfit she had spent considerable time designing in her old clothes-making studio – black trousers and top, thin black gloves, even a black headpiece to conceal their faces when needed, all very soft and mobile. The only difference between them was that his trousers were lose and baggy, hers skin-tight leggings. Exactly why she had done it like that, he didn't know – unless it was some deference to old fashions from before the world had changed. But either way, dressed like this, they ought to have melted into the dark as though they weren't there.

But instead she was an area of night that was just a bit too dark to be true.

He shook his head.

After a long minute, she flitted into motion again and joined him, crouching down and briefly pressing her face against his arm.

"I could see you far too clearly," he said.

She nodded, listened and looked one last time, then stood up with a stretch. "Yeah," she muttered, "this isn't working. I'm going to have to do some more designing, aren't I?" He could feel her slow grin, even in the darkness. "What a chore."

Since it seemed there were no other human beings anywhere near, they finally shifted to a park bench and sat down, removing their masks with some relief. In the silence that hung over London, perhaps its most defining feature now, there seemed time to think again, and in that sense it was beautiful. Jess ran her fingers through her short cropped hair – practical and efficient rather than aesthetic – trying to smooth it down in an odd gesture of vanity that he recognised as lingering from the days before London had changed. She hadn't worn makeup since the event had happened, hadn't worn any high-attention clothes, hadn't even used a razor – all of which had come with a sigh of relief, if anything. But still the old instincts sometimes lingered. Giving up on her hair, she almost unconsciously shuffled up close and he welcomed her, slipping an arm round her waist. This was the kind of simple affectionate gesture that he really appreciated, especially at times like this. It sometimes seemed as though it was the only surviving warmth in the world.

Another moth passed his face in a pale blur and he waved at it absently. Startled, the insect swung away and settled on a nearby tree trunk.

And vanished.

He stared at the spot where it had been. Even though he knew where it was, he couldn't make out the slightest trace of it in the low light. It definitely had better camouflage than they did.

"You got your torch?" he asked.

"Yeah but . . ."

"Let's have it a moment."

She handed it over reluctantly. "Careful," she said. "That hunter might still be looking for us."

He flashed it on and aimed it at the tree, leaning over to look. And even then it took a moment to find it – a small arrow shaped object blended in perfectly with the bark, wings folded and totally still. It was a light grey-brown, marked with bold fuzzy bands of what might have been chestnut. He looked at it thoughtfully.

"That insect is making a mockery of us," he said. "And you know – it isn't black. I suppose there's not much in nature that is black for camouflage, when you think about it."

"Hum – you saying I should design something that looks like that moth?"

"Maybe. If there's one thing in the world that knows how to hide, it's insects." He snapped the torch off again and leaned back. "They look like what they live on. Green or brown, bark coloured, bird shit coloured, dead leaf coloured, soil coloured . . . We live in the city, so . . ."

"There must be some brown fabrics in the shop downstairs," she said. "Maybe even camo pattern."

He nodded. "Yeah – though I was wondering . . ." He flashed the torch on and again illuminated the small insect. The patterns on it were bold and striking when you focussed on them, but they existed to make it look less like an object than like the boundary between objects, or several objects, or part of an object – sending the eye in odd directions. "It's using fake shadows," he said. "Breaking up the shape. Maybe we could do something similar?"

She examined it in silence for a moment. "Okay – let's think about this," she said. "You're the naturalist. How would you go and break up the human body in that sort of way?"

The torch flicked off. He thought for a moment. What were the most obvious parts of the human form? Maybe the head – and maybe the hips, where the legs come together, where the body bends. It's the bit most movement revolves around after all and we can't help but move or stand in certain ways. And of course – the top-bottom divide that comes with so many of our clothes is deeply engrained in our brains.

"I see diagonals," he said with a smile. "Here . . ."

He traced a long diagonal up her body from the knee on one side to under her arm on the other.

"And here." A second line bisected her face and shoulder. "And no belt line."

"When we get home, I will give you some of my design templates and you can draw it? Camouflage suit version two."

"Yes, sure . . ."

But then there was a faint movement in the dark and they both froze. A figure had stepped into the park. It wasn't the same figure as before – it wasn't even the same kind of figure. Instead it looked confused, standing tall but staring around with eyes wide and gleaming. It stood out like a white ghost in the dark, as far from camouflaged as it was possible to be – and that was because it was naked.

"It's one of them," Jess whispered. "Maybe it . . . maybe she saw the torchlight."

They watched in silence. Even in the dark, it was clear that there was something nebulously wrong with her – the way she stood in the middle of the pavement, elegant yet looking around with small slow movements as though high or almost asleep. Then she slowly turned around and made her way off again into the dark, pausing to lean down and peer nervously at a 'keep off the grass' notice before walking away down the very centre of the paved path as though afraid even the slightest veer to the side would doom her.

A figure from a Delvaux painting withdrawing into oblivion.

There was a long and gloomy silence.

"Let's go," she said at last. "Let's see if our rucksacks are still where we left them. You never know."

They left the park, still keeping a wary eye out, and walked back – back through the estate and the suburban streets, back among the parked cars and lightless windows, back to the area of this particular bit of London that might be called its centre, where the largely stripped and looted shops and the railway station were. There was no sign of the hunter anywhere, but there were figures. Naked figures. First one – then another. Then more, all with that half-asleep and bewildered look to them, even as they stood tall and curiously graceful among the old brickwork or glass facades, familiar shop signs and empty shelves. The word noble might even have been applied, in some strange blank-eyed and dreamlike way. It was a scene that still felt utterly strange – a night city full of naked or semi-naked figures, somehow rendered even stranger now by their own contrasting black forms passing among them.

They had come to call these figures the *wanderers,* since that was what they seemed to do. The wanderers and the hunters – the hunters and the hunted – ever since the city had crashed into violence and insanity. They had both long accepted that they would never really know why this was or what had happened. All you could say was that something had gone wrong. Some snap had occurred. Not from without, as far as they could tell – it wasn't a disease, but something in the mind. The early days had been a fog of nightmarish images that made no sense in the context of modern London. Violent chaos as those who had survived unchanged had little choice but to fight back against an outpouring of madness and what looked like hate. It even seemed familiar on some level, maybe because you could always feel slight hints of it in the lower deeps of the human psyche. Everywhere, regardless of politics or inclination. These days it seemed to have faded, but the roles were still preserved. The wanderers were still occasionally dangerous and the hunters still hunted. And every so often, one still encountered fresh bodies lying in the London streets among the familiar scattering of bones.

There was a small group of them standing forlornly at a road crossing, staring up and down the street – all naked and all standing with that same tall yet broken nobility – one even carrying a lantern in which a small flame flickered, which was a little unusual. The faint light reflected off their skin, giving it a painting-like sense of unreality, which was only increased by the sight of the bare human skull lying against the wall. Jess and Jay watched them warily as they approached, ready to slip away if any of them started coming in their direction. But they didn't.

"They're waiting for the lights to change," she said under her breath. "Waiting for the little green man."

He stared up at the dead traffic lights with a quiet sigh, skin prickling. The light was not going to turn green again any time soon. "It doesn't make sense," he said, half to himself. "Why should they still be stuck in one fairly trite dictated behaviour yet completely forget another?"

Jess just shrugged and they pressed on, passing the group and crossing the road. The naked figures stared after them in complete bemusement – confused expressions on their faces that were almost heart-breaking, as though the two of them had floated into the air. It was a relief to reach the other side and step round the corner into the next street, a wrecked estate agents cutting the sight from their eyes.

Eventually the wanderers would wander away again back the way they had come – rather that than jaywalk.

Here, the massive shape of a railway bridge framed the world, casting a deep moonshadow. They hurried under it and back into the light. More dead shops processed past, wrecked windows gleaming jagged. A small supermarket, now almost picked clean – a pizza place that was a cave of darkness – a café, chairs and tables strewn around in devastation. And then tall narrow residential housing hidden behind scraps of garden, and what had happened to the people living here was anybody's guess, though the occasional scattering of human bones maybe said enough.

"I should get hold of some *No unauthorised persons beyond this point* signs," he said. "Put them on our door. We'd be impregnable."

Jess frowned. "That's just about weird enough to work . . . except that it would probably attract the hunters. You know how they seem to take a delight in busting in anywhere they shouldn't."

"True."

"Could put one on our bedroom door though," she said with a grin.

"Or hey, maybe you should build some nice red *Do not touch* signs into our outfits. Could keep them hidden – like those moths with hidden eye spots that they flash at predators."

She gave a laugh. "Oh boy – I wish I could have come up with that one back in the days when there were still runways to run on. Though I shudder to think what the what the connotations would have been back then."

The residential houses soon changed to shops again and now they were back at the point where all this started. It was immediately obvious that the rucksacks full of food had gone – and it was easy enough to guess where. No doubt some hunters would be very pleased with their little bonus. Jess swore softly

"Dawn soon," she muttered gloomily. "Let's go home. No sense pushing it. Then we can get on with designing – and say goodbye to these damn black suits."

He looked at her – sleek black hole in the night that she was. And yes, black was the crucial mistake. Black that added to the darkness of the world rather than blended into it. Black that formed a hole – a moment of unnatural and cold dark that the eye could be tuned to. All the black archetypes – the black-clad assassin, the black ninja, the thief in the black skinsuit, all trying to be so cool and superlative, maybe they were all built on a lie. The dark and the black were very different things.

14

Take the dark on its own terms, one might say. *You can't fight the dark – you have to embrace it.* And maybe that went further than they had ever thought.

*

Jess came in, struggling under a load of rolls of fabric from the shop downstairs. Browns. There were shiny browns and dull browns, red-browns and green-browns and grey browns, light browns and dark browns, sandy browns and stony browns, patterned browns and plain browns . . .

"Mind if I switch to dawn light?" she asked.

"Is it that late?" he asked sleepily, looking up from the template he had been working on. The latest of many, at least some of which were lying screwed up on the floor. These templates were familiar things – simple line drawings of a naked girl, front and back. It seemed a ridiculous image – legs so long it looked more like a cartoon. How the heck were you supposed to design something for the human body using a figure that looked as though it had been stretched on a medieval rack? She had managed it though, back in the days when there were still people in the world interested in such things. She had managed it very well indeed.

He sat back with a stretch as she hurried round snuffing the candles, bringing a darkness that was more intense than anything outside. Then the flash of a torch and she was taking down the blackout panels from the windows. The grey morning light was quite a shock after the warm candle glow and he shielded his eyes for a moment. Morning was a time for retiring from the world and barricading themselves inside. Hiding like moths themselves from those that came out during the day. Directly outside the windows and a few diagonal metres below was one of the elevated railways striding through the city on brick arches

– now silent, the timetables, wires and booked paths all dead. That viaduct was good company and a ladder stood propped against the wall in most of the back rooms in case access was needed. The railway tracks were a fine path through the city these days. They were protected by signs and fences better than pretty much any other place. Not one single wanderer had ever been seen there – and even the hunters seemed to have no use for them.

She settled down with her pile of fabric rolls and began sorting them. Anything too shiny was rejected and tossed aside. Then she went through them again quickly twizzling the fabric in her fingers, and this time anything too noisy was rejected. He watched with interest. Any time she was handling fabric, she was worth watching. She was like a virtuoso violinist.

"How's it going?" she called at last.

He picked up the last design. "Well – I've got something. Not sure what though."

She dropped the fabric and leaned over him, studying the drawing with interest.

"Is that a onesie?" she asked. "Or a skinsuit? You've got a seam running all the way from thigh to underarm. Tricky."

He shrugged.

"No idea – I am just drawing shapes. After that, it's up to you."

"Okay," she said, picking up the sheet. "Fuck it – I wish I had my old design software. This is going to be hard. But I can only try."

He yielded the desk to her and watched with a sleepy smile as she dragged out more templates and started sketching. Occasionally jabbing at the calculator.

They had moved here above the fabric shop soon after the city had changed, only too happy to escape the tiny apartment they had shared before. It had been a life of barely controlled insanity as time ticked by – her clothes-making studio in the bedroom, his computer building and repair workshop in the

16

kitchen. That was the old London, and predictably enough, health was failing, as it seemed was sanity. And right there was the beautiful irony to everything that had happened. For the first time ever, there was a blissful sense of space in life that almost made the apocalypse of human civilization seem worthwhile – but now they finally had the room to do things, there was no one left to do them for. The London alt fashion scene was totally dead and certainly nobody wanted their computer fixed anymore. He had left his computer equipment in the old house, but she couldn't bring herself to get rid of all her clothes though. This room, designated the work room, was full of them – rail after rail. The best of her old stock that had once been sold everywhere from Camden market to Australia. In those times when there was nothing to do, she would get them out, put them on and perform bizarre one-person shows for him, or drag him into it and they would mess around with them together. Her lack of makeup and severe hair made little difference – indeed without the paint job she only seemed more real, more of a body that was being adorned rather than an undefined thing trying to pretend it wasn't flesh. These outfits had once startled the alternate fashion events around north and east London – Hackney, the Wick, Islington, Camden – stalking the runway in what might have been an abandoned or converted factory or warehouse somewhere in the city. Dressing up like this, she seemed to become a different person – something much sharper. And both now and then, the sight of her doing what she did best was close to awe-inspiring.

Somehow that seemed both melancholy and beautiful now.

"I think I might head to bed," he said at last. "Do you need me for anything?"

"Mmm – no. I will join you when I've done this." Jess hesitated and looked round. "Um – any thoughts yet about getting some kind of solar rig on the roof."

His heart sank. "If I could just run a few internet searches," he said, trying to be humorous.

She nodded, not betraying any frustration. "It would be nice to get the electric sewing machine going, that's all. It would be so good if y. . . if we could work out something as useful as an electricity supply. We could get the fridge going again as well."

"Yeah, I bet it would," he said gloomily as she settled back down at her desk. "Computers are a long way from home electronics . . . I'll have to try and find a book on it."

He turned to the window, watching the city under the morning light. It was hard not to feel down. What was he good at? A certain knowledge of natural history was proving useful – helpful for identifying edible plants and hunting for the remaining London wildlife – but that was about all. He wasn't even particularly fit or strong.

In pop culture, the cliché of apocalypses and collapses of civilization always seemed to be some kind of quazi-millitary/survivalist fantasy of blazing guns, maybe thundering round in big cars – the collapse of society finally giving you the freedom to rampage. And the hunters seemed happy enough to go along with that here as well. But even as the hunters fought over reserves of ammo and petrol, they inevitably dwindled and what use would either be soon? At least some form of sustainability was now vital – a matter of basic imminent survival. Instead of cars, maybe sailing would be better – a skill with handling and building boats. Or bicycles? Both were far more useful in this world. Or instead of guns, how about lapidary – knapping a lethal blade or arrowhead out of a Thames flint or a broken bottle? All somewhat unfashionable occupations, not that high up in the perception of some wannabe zombie hunter.

And now clothes design? It would appear so. Clothes were important. Clothes were *always* important – pretty much any usage of them, even their absence. Clothes were a language, including when trying to say 'I'm not here'. Including when trying to stop yourself dying.

"Go to bed," Jess said with a smile, before those thoughts could settle too deeply. "I'll be through soon – too tired to do much more of this now."

He gave her a wan smile and left the room.

*

When the two new camouflage suits were finally finished, after much testing and trying, fitting and stitching, the result was nothing if not impressive – a somewhat bizarre but effective creation in subtle and dull brown shades that might once have been worthy of the runway. And in deference to years of working practice, she couldn't resist giving it a formal presentation. Since he was the only audience though, it turned into what might be called a reverse striptease – putting on one part of it after another and happily showing it off in a comical parody of a fashion show. It was the middle of the night and they had lit every single candle they had. The room positively blazed as she pranced around, showing off.

First came a simple pair of dark brown trousers made of soft loose material covered with rough patterning – ordinary enough and hugging her body comfortably. Over that came something much more unusual. It was loose yet hitched up round her in a surprisingly elegant way – a baggy top that segued into an irregular pair of shorts with hems ranging from hip to knee level and no line in the belt area. The colours were complicated yet subtle, areas of patterned fabric and monochrome, as well as two of the diagonal colour-changes that he had drawn, cutting the body clean in half in a grand sweep. She had made them by meticulously layering thin strips of material in an irregular band that flowed round her body, fading one area of colour to another. The result was simultaneously a confusing patchwork and something very tightly controlled – a muddle and a thing of beauty not quite like anything he had ever seen before.

Finally there was the mask, which she pulled on last, striking a pose that only an alt-fashion model could possibly get her body into. It covered her entire head and this also featured a diagonal seam as he had scribbled it, as though half her head was casting a shadow – a not-quite-vertical dark/light divide from her left cheek and bisecting her right eyehole before looping round her head. The colours of the mask corresponded to the colours of her shoulders and neck, breaking up the shape very effectively.

No black anywhere.

"That is absolutely terrifying," he said, grinning. And she was. She looked seriously strange – the mask especially might have been added to the canon of great horror movie costumes – but crucially the shapes that the different colours made, though distinct, weren't human.

"Shut your eyes and count to ten," she said, putting the candles out and opening the blackout panels. Moonlight streamed in, bathing her and turning her into a strange patterned heap. He obeyed, listening as she darted off to some new location in the room with a giggle. Footstep footstep – silence . . . faint sound of fabric . . . more silence.

Reaching ten in his head, he opened his eyes again and looked round, straining to find her.

"Okay," he said at last. "I know you're there but . . . where the heck are you?"

No answer. Just the faintest of faint rustlings of fabric. Even giving up looking for a Jess-shaped figure and focussing instead on anything in the room that was different to how he remembered it didn't help. It was a faintly maddening sensation – his sharpened instincts trying to function, but not quite able to. If it wasn't a game, it could have been seriously creepy.

A faint scuff from somewhere and he turned round sharply. "I can hear you," he said, pacing round the room. "Can't see you though. Where . . ?"

More silence. A flicker of movement and he spun round, only for something to come straight out of the dark at him in a silent explosion.

"Boo," she yelled in his ear – and grabbed him into a hug. For a moment they wrestled together in the dark, banging into clothes rails and furniture, laughing hugely, then he tripped over something and they landed in a heap. Even with her sitting astride him, he could hardly see her. He could see something – see movement and feel her weight, but the eye was having a hard time interpreting it as any kind of human figure.

Then she tugged the mask off, and her face floated into view. "There you go," she said, leaning down and giving him a kiss. "Does it work?"

"It sure does," he said.

"Brown is definitely the new black," she said happily. "And if the world ever returns to normal, I will make a fortune with my new line of night camouflage eveningwear. I could probably find ways to make this quieter, but hey – it seems good. Come on," she cried. "Put yours on again and let's go out and test them properly."

*

The ladder slid out of the window until it touched the parapet of the railway viaduct, then hooked into place securely. It was a shallow angle – not that far off horizontal. This was always a rather fiddly operation and an area where Jess could show him up completely. She hopped onto the ladder in the dark and happily crawled along it on all fours, in spite of the downwards incline and the empty rucksack on her shoulders. He followed rather less gracefully, shuffling along the wobbling horror as best he could. Below, the slot between the elevated tracks and the building seemed very dark indeed. There was a tiny courtyard there – a space of old concrete and abandoned furniture – but from here it looked as though it plunged down forever. It was enough to induce vertigo and as always it was a relief to set foot on the railway line in a crunch of ballast.

"That never seems to get any easier," he muttered, straightening his rucksack.

They were wearing the suits but not the masks, which were carefully stashed in a pocket. There was no sense restricting their vision until it was needed. But as they walked, they gave the impression of two disembodied faces drifting through the dark, which didn't help the railway line feel any less ghostly. He felt a distinct prickle as he paced along from sleeper to sleeper – something that was probably never going to go away, no matter how often they walked here. The tracks that used to thrum and shake beneath the London commuter trains definitely occupy a special place in the mind – an electrical forbidden zone – one of the great taboos – a keep out here be dragons place hammered into you from an early age. It was easy to see why the wanderers wouldn't come here.

They made their way along the line, past the dense and clustering buildings of East London – narrow houses of murky brown brick with steep complex rooves and tiny little sinkholes of yards and sheds below. Down there, the familiar detritus of the city still lingered – abandoned rubbish in the public areas, abandoned possessions in the private. Forlorn garden furniture left in a space of a couple of metres square – children's play equipment, toys, rooves colonised by garden ornaments and dead pot plants. The occasional stranger thing like the scrawled street art – mostly white tags but also a few more elaborate things, like a stroppy purple monkey face or highly stylised white teeth set in yellow and pink gums. Now there was no one to clean them off, maybe they would linger for quite a while in this new world, until the elements finally wore them down to nothing. Or there was the life-size cardboard cut-out of some Japanese cartoon character that stared out of one window, now just visible in the darkness. Jay could remember that from the days of riding the train here – and he had certainly never expected to be seeing it on foot.

They didn't say much as they walked. Something about this environment, not to mention Jess's near invisibility, was urging silence. It would have only taken a few minutes to reach the destination they had chosen by train but now, on foot, it seemed a long walk. Railways were places where you were supposed to move fast, not slow. They passed a dark station – then another, with one or two naked figures sitting on the platform, watching them as they passed.

"Just round the bend, I think," Jay said at last.

And it was. As the third station came into view though, they drifted to a stop. There were figures visible on the platform – rather more this time. At least ten. All naked though one seemed to be carrying what looked like a silk scarf draped over her shoulders – all picked out white and dark and other shades in the moonlight.

And even here, human bones could be seen, an occasional presence on the mundane slabs of the platform.

If Paul Delvaux had ever set his works in grubby and multicultural East London, it might look a bit like this. As strange a sight as any they had seen.

"They're waiting for a train," she whispered. "I wonder how long they've been there?"

"Now what?"

There was a silence – then they quietly started walking again.

As they approached the platforms, the figures began to gather, watching them with a somewhat chilling fascination – and as the sloping concrete rose up and levelled like walls on either side, as they continued walking along the tracks between them, the wanderers followed, keeping pace almost a metre above.

"They can't come down here," she whispered. "I feel like I'm on the runway again at the worst show of my life. Question is, how do we get up? Just climb up and make a dash for it?"

"I suppose so – if we're fast we ought to be okay."

At regular intervals, there was a step made of bricks and marked with grubby white paint set against the edge of the platform to allow people to scramble up. It was a lot better than trying to haul yourself up unassisted. It is hard to grasp how high railway platforms are until you are on the tracks below them. They approached one quickly but cautiously. The station exit was not far away.

"Okay," she said. "Just up and out, right?"

"Uh-huh."

The figures were already gathering around. They seemed fascinated by these two rebels daring to venture where they could not. The camouflage suits were surprisingly flexible – clothes you could move in, and he had no trouble bounding up onto the step and then onto the platform itself. Jess was following and he stepped aside to give her room. Then her foot slipped and she stumbled down again with a gasp. He hurried forward and grabbed her hand, hauling her up – but time had been wasted – and naked figures were all around them now, poking at them and tugging at their clothes. The two stared at them uneasily. To get to the exit they would have to push past – and that was not appealing. There were already hints of wariness and aggression in the crowd. Individually, the wanderers were not very dangerous, but in groups things could be much nastier. If one did something, others would follow – so if one decided to attack, even if it was just like a confused child . . .

A brief exchange of glances.

"Fuck it," she muttered. He edged along the platform slowly, trying to find a way round them – she stepped back though, then jumped down again onto the ballast with a crunch. The step was totally blocked now by the crowd and she stared round unhappily. The next step was a few dozen yards further down –

24

further away from the exit. It was a crazy situation – not immediately threatening but with the logistics of a nightmare to it. He stared round at the crowd – and in a way they were beautiful, as any nude was. Maybe it was because they stood there with so little self-consciousness – standing tall rather than hunched and ashamed – curious faces gleaming in all the skin colours the body was capable of. Faces that were not by any means devoid of expression and life.

Maybe that dreamlike feeling helped because right then an idea flashed fully formed into his mind.

"Wait a minute," he said, tugging at his top. "Strip."

"Huh?"

Jess stared up at him blankly as he struggled out of the camouflage suit. It was tricky – he was not used to the way this thing held together yet, and the hands poking and pulling at him were only making things worse – but once he got it off, his skin prickling hugely in the cold air, it seemed to have the desired effect. Something had shifted in the atmosphere of the crowd – he was no longer quite so interesting.

Unfortunately though, that meant they had all focussed on Jess now. They were clustering at the platform edge in an unbroken line and he was starting to worry what might happen if one of them fell down.

"Get 'em off," he hissed sharply.

"Oh – oh, right . . ."

Standing between the railway tracks, she finally began dragging her own suit off, switching from almost invisible to as exposed as you can be – not camouflaged now but painfully pale in the moonlight. The two stared at each other – then she quietly dropped the armful of clothes over the rail and stood there frozen. The way she was standing was very different to the wanderers and she looked agonisingly fragile and scared rather than tall and noble – but it was working. The crowd seemed to be relaxing a bit – still staring down but the pressure reducing, some starting to drift away again.

The sight of her standing so very naked in such a harsh environment sent a huge burst of prickling over his skin. Even when you are used to someone and know what they look like, seeing them like this in such a strange context can make them look entirely alien. She gave him a worried stare – but there was nothing to do but wait. Time slowly dispersed the crowd, scattering them around the platform again.

Finally she handed her clothes up to him, then he grabbed her hand and hauled her up at last.

"Gawd sake," she muttered shakily. "Can we get out of here?"

With massive tension and a prickle of cold air, the two walked slowly through the scattered crowd towards the exit, clutching the camouflage suits and rucksacks – but there was no further trouble. It was a strange sensation – to be rendered safe by something that felt as vulnerable as nakedness.

"Fucking bizarre." Jess muttered as they passed through the ticket gates. The station was trashed for some reason, ticket gates open or ripped out entirely, many of the signs and notices missing – which no doubt explained the number of wanderers on the platform. Outside in the street, everything seemed quiet and they hastily slipped round a corner – then ended up leaning against a wall in a massive hug. He could feel her trembling slightly.

"Oh boy – that was crazy," she muttered.

He shook his head. "What is it with them?" he said, repeating an old mystification. "It doesn't make any sense. They can't help but obey signs and can't go on the railway – but they seem to have totally forgotten what clothes are . . . I don't get it."

"There's different levels going on here. Maybe clothes are a different kind of fiction to *keep off the railway line*." There was a silence. "Killing people too," she added with a gloomy grimace. "There's no signs about those. No immediate codes or rulebooks."

He nodded slowly. "You remember how we always used to worry that overregulation actually lead to people obsessed with the letter of the law but totally useless at making moral judgements?" he murmured. "I wonder . . ."

She gave him a weird look.

"I'm not sure I'd call clothes 'moral'," she said, smiling.

"Yeah – but in terms of mechanics, how the brain works . . ." He shrugged, losing track of the thoughts. "It's going to be interesting in the winter, that's all I can say."

"Yeah – well, whatever they are, we'd better get dressed," she said uneasily. "If a hunter ran across us like this we'd probably have a bullet in the brain in about five seconds."

That was true, he realised with a chill, glancing up and down the street. Everything seemed quiet but they dressed again with some relief. Bare skin against harsh brick and concrete was a strange paring – another wholly new and rather surreal experience for this city.

"Fuck it," she muttered.

"What?"

"They've torn it."

It was hard to see in the dark, but there was a glimmer of white skin. The main part had been ripped open along a seam, from hips to armpit.

"Can we find somewhere to stop? Where I can put the light on for a bit? I can fix this in a few minutes, at least enough to get me home."

They scanned the nearby buildings, looking for somewhere that might be safe – ideally of no interest to either the hunters or the hunted. It was an ordinary east London street of smaller shops, most with the familiar smashed windows and bare shelves showing like the skeletal remains that also filled the world. Fast food joints accompanied them – even more ghostly, with the last of the fried chicken or kebabs rotted away leaving grimy metal and yet more bones. It all seemed quiet, but there was nothing that felt totally safe here.

"I could use a moment to take a few deep breaths as well," she muttered. "I am feeling fucking jittery."

"Me too. Let's try a side street."

This was more residential in nature but still with a few shops and other facilities. An estate agent – mouthpiece of a gruesome empire of housing finally brought to dust. A Chinese takeaway. A wine shop, totally stripped bare. And then something else.

"Bookshop," she said, pointing. "Think the hunters read?"

They stared in cautiously. Aside from the smashed in door, everything looked reasonably intact and they entered, stepping over the broken glass with care to avoid noise. It was a small and presumably once independent shop, with shelves mostly still filled – art books, the trendier side of fiction, intellectual pondering and the instructive, self-help and cookery etc. etc.

"I wonder if there's a section on electronics for beginners," he said.

"You should have a look. Let's – check it over first though." She quietly pulled the mask over her head.

"Of course."

That was standard. If you enter an unfamiliar place, the first thing you need to do is make sure you know the layout, know what's there, know who's there, and know how to get out of it again.

Just in case.

With that in mind, they performed a quick search, listening carefully.

Most of the shop was pretty much undamaged. Near the broken door, however, some of the display was succumbing to the elements, pages warped and mildewed – and further in a skull was staring up at them from the floor, surrounded by a several metre wide halo of stained and rotted books. No doubt the rotting of the flesh was easily transmitted to the paper around it. They stared at it gloomily for a moment.

At the back of the shop, one doorway led further into the building. After some cautious listening, Jess opened it a crack

28

and listened some more. But the silence seemed absolute. Eventually she pulled it open, revealing a small and excruciatingly dark room beyond. A glimmer of moonlight revealed another door to the outside and a small window, as well as dark shapes of furniture. That was all.

She darted across to the other door and tried it. It was open, but revealed nothing more than a small alleyway and a further gate, also standing half open.

"Okay," Jess said. "I guess this is as good as anywhere. Two ways to run if needed. Will you keep a lookout for me? I won't be long. I just don't want this thing flapping around. And," she added with a small laugh, "I don't want my ice-white tits showing up like a bloody beacon when I am trying to hide."

"Okay," he said, smiling.

He pulled the door into the shop closed behind them to prevent any light escaping in that direction, then put his ear to it, keeping up a general auditory scan of the area. She dropped her bag and rummaged in it, pulling out a torch and snapping it on.

"Thanks. Now I'll just . . . woah."

She had frozen completely at what was revealed by that stabbing ray of light.

Jay was also surprised, so much so that he forgot to breathe for a moment. The dark room had revealed little but the basics before – just hulking shapes of dark on dark. And for a long time, Jess stood there, aiming the torch in silence. Then she rummaged in her bag again and pulled out a small lantern powered by a little tea-light candle.

Its light filled the whole room and Jay quietly sat down on the untidy bed by the door – and still there didn't seem anything to say.

The room was filled with art.

The walls were covered with it – canvases rested on easels and more were stacked around against the walls. And on the canvases, on the white walls themselves – the most extraordinary fantastical scenes. Vivid colourful surrealism but with somewhat bloody and tormented overtones. Hints of the monstrous in figures and landscapes. One painting in particular, so huge that it needed two easels to support it, dragged the eyes. It was unfinished, and its extraordinary complexity suggested that it had been in progress for a long time. In it, two massive columns of people, one naked, one clothed, were walking away into what could only be called a double sunset – two suns in the sky hanging just above the horizon. A maze of fences constrained the naked ones, while a wasteland of fire surrounded the clothed in equally regimented lines. The nearest naked figures showed massive bloody holes where their hearts would be – while the corresponding clothed walkers showed gruesome holes in their heads, with fragments of brain trickling and dribbling out and down onto their shoulders. The colours were also suggestive – a blazing red sun for the clothed, a cool-looking blue and green one for the naked. Though of course, if you knew astronomy, blue stars were actually hotter and the radiance seemed dazzling. There were some very definite keys here, obviously.

It was also clear that this wasn't old. There was a faint tang of acrylic paints in the air, now the nose knew what to smell for. There were jars of murky water – and some of the paint lingering on the pallet was still wet. This was not left over from before the world changed – this was now. There were signs of habitation here too. There was an old bed in one corner, a huge mirror, a now presumably useless microwave oven, a washbasin, various boxes etc. It was a small, cramped depressing space, little more than a camp – the sort of space that far too many Londoners had been forced to live in in the days before . . .

Jess was starting to collect herself. "I'm not sure we should be here," she whispered. "But now we are – just give me a few moments." She reached into her rucksack again and extracted her sewing kit. Then she climbed out of the top part of the suit and settled down half-naked to work on it. He watched her briefly, then stared round the room again, feeling suddenly melancholy at the world that had moved on so utterly. Why were the most precious things always lost or rendered irrelevant first? No more books now – not for the foreseeable future anyway. No more novels. No more intricate and complex musical works. No more luxury of beauty for its own sake. No more eyes to see or care about this painting. And it was depressing how keen some people seemed to be to embrace that, as though it validated some deep deep ugliness within themselves, where only the practical ruled.

He was deep in those thoughts when there was a sound behind him – something in the shop beyond the door. They both froze and he jumped up in horror, swearing at himself for forgetting to listen.

But there was only a second before the door opened.

Jess spun round, coming face to face with a naked figure. Male – untidy pale hair receding slightly in spite of his young age and revealing a huge forehead above haunted eyes.

For a moment there was a completely frozen silence, while Jess clutched her clothes to herself. Jay was watching warily, ready to step in if needed. One person, one young man didn't look too threatening, but it payed to be careful.

For a moment, the figure gave them a forlorn and dreamy stare, then abruptly plunged forward with a faint cry, mad to repel this intrusion into what was presumably his private place. Jay also dived forwards. Jess tried to back away, but in the process managed to drop the clothes. She staggered back against the wall in her soft trousers, topless and anything but camouflaged – but the figure had come to a stop again. Almost as though a force field had gone up around her. He stared at her bare skin, all aggression draining away.

Jess stared back, trying to work it out – and something was being communicated through the space between them. Something that felt deafening in the deep silence. Jay could see it clearly. Jess was slowly relaxing.

Then the figure reached out a hand – very gingerly, closing the gap between them and aiming to touch her shoulder. And more communication was being exchanged – like an invisible harp string vibrating, changing the shape of the silence. And finally, she reached out her arms in an inviting gesture – and gathered him into a hug.

Jay watched feeling a dull amazement. Astonishingly enough, it seemed to be working. He hugged her back, tears streaming down his face and a jittery tension in his body.

"It's okay," she whispered, rubbing his back.

It was a hug that looked as though it could have gone on forever – indeed he seemed to want it to. It was Jess who had to break it eventually, though with some awkwardness – gently disentangling his hands. She stepped away – but that proved to be a mistake. He gave a wail and clutched at her – then a screech of frustration, like a kid watching something he desperately needs withdrawing out of reach. He lashed out at her – but it was barely more than a slap, and Jess merely blinked and grasped his hand . . .

And then a shot rang out from somewhere and the artist keeled over instantly, a bloody hole in the side of his face.

Jess closed her eyes . . .

"What the fuck?" The hunter regarded them with cautious bewilderment, gun aimed at Jay now. "Who are you? You have five seconds to identify yourselves or . . ."

"Identify ourselves?" Jay echoed, his voice shrill. "How? Why?"

"Are you human?"

"Of course we bloody are."

"What's six times five?"

"Huh? Um . . ." He thought frantically, his mind frozen. *Fifty five? No . . .* "Thirty?" he ventured at last.

"What's the third line of the Lord's Prayer?"

Oh gawd . . .

Again he tried desperately to summon the information from whatever deep part of the mind it was stored in. Somewhat miraculously, he found it.

"Thy kingdom come," he managed at last.

"Name three positions in a football team," he barked.

"What?" Jay cried, finally losing patience. "How the heck should I know?"

Jess finally opened her eyes again then, staring from the crumpled figure on the floor to the newcomer and back again.

"What are you pointing that thing at us for?" she demanded quietly.

"You are – still whole?"

"Of course," she said. "Can't you tell?"

"Then why are you naked?"

She glanced down at herself as though finally remembering that she was only dressed in her trousers. "We were surprised," she said coldly.

"At what? Do I even want to know?"

Her cold look became even colder. Without a word, she reached for her half-mended clothes.

"Hold it," he said smoothly, twitching the gun. "Don't move."

"Why not?"

"Who are you with?" the hunter continued. He touched the abandoned rucksacks with his toe. "If you're here to nick our grub, the results could be very very painful."

"Your food?" Jay asked warily.

"Of course. This is our fucking area. Where are you from? The Dalston gang? Stratford?"

The two exchanged glances.

"We're not with any group," she said at last.

The hunter raised his eyebrows. "Bollocks," he growled. "Not many strays left now – and the ones that are should probably just be put down for their own good. Turn round."

"What?"

"Do it."

With a bewildered look, Jess turned her back and the hunter studied her closely.

"What are you looking for?" Jay asked.

"Tattoo," he said. "You ain't Dalston, at least. "Clothes."

"What about them?"

"Give – me – your – clothes," he said with exaggerated patience. "Let's have a look at them. Let's see what identifying marks you got." He gestured Jay into the centre of the room and stared at him, eyebrows up. "What the heck kind of dumb pansy getup are you wearing? Is that some kind of . . . of . . . what is it? I don't even know where to begin."

There was a silence. Jay honestly had no idea what to say. The hunter was wearing a military style field jacket – oddly enough in desert 3-colour camo pattern – and a pair of black trousers that looked as though they came from a cheap suit. An incongruous mix. It was hard to say what he could have been in his previous life. His slightly arrogant tone possibly suggested a low-level manager or shop owner, the sort used to being on top of his tiny little chain of command.

Jess meanwhile had quietly taken her suit and was putting it on.

"I told you," she said shortly. "Not with any group. Not from around here either. Just visiting."

The hunter pulled a face. "I'll say this," he muttered, "I can't imagine any group dressed as dumb as that. I dunno – this city just gets worse and worse. You had better come with me. We'll sort it out back home – and for your sake, I hope you are solos. We'll forgive you stealing our food if you join us and make yourselves useful."

Jay and Jess exchanged glances a second time.

"Alright," she said quietly with a tiny shrug. "Let's go. I guess it's better that way."

The hunter lowered the gun to his side and shepherded them back into the main shop, flashing the torch around. Then out into the empty street.

Looking back on it, Jay was obscurely proud of how little communication was needed for what happened next. No signal was given, no one took the lead. When the moment was right, when the hunter was beginning to make up his mind that all was well, gun back in holster, they both simply started running. It was as if their two minds were meshed together so well that some kind of telepathy was taking place.

"Hey," the hunter yelled, angry and astonished, but they ignored him. "Come back here – what are you playing at?" There was a gunshot that made his skin freeze, though it was probably merely into the air. "You're either with us or against us," he yelled stupidly. "And you won't fucking get far, you know . . ."

The two darted into a side street and finally came to a stop, jumping into an overgrown garden and plunging into a shadowy corner.

"Time to test these fucking pansy suits of mine," she said, dragging on her mask again. He quickly did likewise.

They froze still, hidden by bushes, trying to find a position that was comfortable enough to last but not so relaxed as to give them away. He could feel her heart racing at extraordinary speed.

And it seemed to work. There was a clatter of feet as the hunter passed only a metre or so away, torch flashing, glancing round as he ran, a nasty look on his face. His eyes must have passed right over them in the dark – but he didn't see them. Maybe the flashing dazzle of the torch made it even harder to focus on the shapes of those camouflage suits.

The two finally relaxed and he felt her arm slide round him in a tense and shivery squeeze.

"Ohhhh boy," she muttered. "Now what? Think it's safe to go shopping? Think there's anything left?"

*

The wrecked railway station was easy enough the second time. They simply ran up the stairs and out onto the platform. There were still several wanderers hanging around there, staring at them with the familiar expression of serene yet tragic bemusement. Even with fully loaded rucksacks, it was easy enough to dodge what little reaction there was and to jump down onto the tracks where they couldn't follow – and then they were hurrying into the dark again, until the station was out of sight round a bend and they were alone on the railway viaduct.

"Oh fuck it," she muttered, stopping abruptly. "I need a rest."

She sat down heavily against the wall. Around them, the dark east London buildings clustered like some bizarre form of vegetation or fungal growth, through which the elevated railway had barged, its brick arches like the tread of some great beast frozen in time – in the style of Duchamp's Nude Descending a Staircase, maybe. There was enough light in the air now to see quite well – a bright moon had come out. And it dawned on him then that this was an entirely new sight. London under moonlight. In the old days, the red/orange glow had been continuous, the moon nothing more than a pallid white disk in a glowing haze, totally outshone by the city. But now a silvery light hung over everything – something so ghostly and unique that he was stunned. The dark of the city somehow only seemed more so against that.

Dark . . . but not black. Even now.

"Eventually we are going to have to get out of here, you know," he said at last. "This is just – scavenging. We can catch a few waterbirds and keep scouring the shops for tins and dry stuff but it won't go on forever."

She nodded. "Yeah. Especially with these guys running around everywhere. London is going to become a death trap."

"Uh-huh. And you know . . . I was thinking about something else as well."

"What?"

"The power's out, right? How many automated systems have shut down? All it would take is one major chemical leak or gas explosion and we would have had it."

"I hadn't thought of that," she murmured. There was an uncomfortable silence. "And besides, what is there here for us?"

"I can imagine it now," he muttered. "They'll be fighting amongst themselves, there'll be hierarchy and bullying. All the old ugly parts of humanity on the surface again and hey, welcome back my old repressed friends."

She buried her face in her hands. "I think I prefer the wanderers."

There wasn't much he could say to that – so he contented himself with looking at the moonlight. Jess had pretty much vanished again, he realised, like the moth against the tree trunk. He knew where she was, but he really had to stare to make out any sign of her.

"You ever wonder whether there are actually two types of people," she continued in a low voice. "Two species almost?"

"Hmm?"

"You know – how humanity always seems to want to divide itself into two separate sides of thought – left, right – allies, axis – communist, capitalist – good, evil. Until you just get to the stage where no-one even remembers how the other half thinks or why?"

"Yeah – but . . ." He hesitated. "That's a normal reaction to a blurred world surely? I mean . . . don't we always try and find these massive black and white simplifications?"

"Yes. But why do we have such difference? There has to be an inbuilt duality. And what if that duality had something to do with what happened?"

"How?"

"Well – do you have any idea what kind of mind it was that succumbed to this? And what didn't? I bet anything you like that it won't be random. Are the wanderers the sensitive ones? The caring ones? The ones that hurt most and thought most? Felt most. That guy in the shop was an artist – with real skill."

She was silent for a moment.

"Maybe there really is a group consciousness," she said. "On some shadowy level. And one day it just snapped. *Excuse me sir,*" she said, suddenly putting on a very posh accent, "*but do you happen to have any medicine for a ruptured consciousness?*"

She gave a laugh that he didn't like very much. It sounded a little bit hysterical.

"Maybe, on that day, there was one last news report," she continued, her voice going shrill. "Some last injustice shared round on the news and social networks that was so mindbogglingly stupid and horrible that all the decent humanity just folded up. Decided that was it – can't stand it any longer and bye bye world."

"Um . . ."

Her laughter continued. "Do you have a better idea? And I guess we got what some people always wanted. No more need to make a society that works now. Now there's just a nice group of people to hate and exterminate, no consequences and they don't need to worry about being nice to anyone and *his face was just a foot away from me and I saw it shatter . . .*"

She collapsed into hysterical crying.

He stared at her. For a moment he actually found himself considering what she had said – long enough to wonder *so where does that leave us?* But then reality caught up – at least as far as it ever could. It seemed possible to consider anything in the face of what had happened to the world. When you are walking through a deranged and aggressive Delvaux canvas, any theory seems possible.

He sat down beside her, letting her grab him into a desperate hug.

"I think," he whispered after a long few minutes of silver moonlight, "we should go home. And stay there for a little while. We've got more than enough food for weeks anyway." He paused. "And do some thinking," he added.

"Yeah," she muttered. "I'm sorry, I guess this has been building up for a while."

Except that crying was never a sign of weakness. People needed comfort, needed emotion, and contact, and love, and all the nice warm things – because without them you were nothing. He wanted to find a way to say that, but he wasn't sure how – and soon the moment was lost into the near infinity of thoughts never uttered. He helped her up, well aware of his own hands shaking, and they began to walk along the dark tracks, watching the silver houses of London's East End passing by – wall after wall of dead gleaming windows. Or were they? Who knows who else was living out there in the city? Who knows what lives were continuing as best they could? Where did the wanderers sleep? What drear and regimented bases did the hunters operate?

Take the dark on its own terms. You can't fight the dark – you have to embrace it.

But was that really true? For something as simple as the night, maybe – but for human darkness…?

"You know," she said as they walked, "it would be fairly easy to rig a bike to ride on these rails. You'd just need flanged wheels. The bike could ride on one rail and there could be a – a sort of long stabiliser thing to run on the other rail. Maybe with a small cargo cart. Or no – better, two bikes attached together, luggage carrier slung between them."

He nodded thoughtfully, relieved at the new tone of interest in her voice. "Could maybe add some rubber strips to make it quieter," he suggested.

"Or even – hey . . . is there any reason we couldn't add a small sail?"

"Within the railway's loading gauge . . ."

He drew a deep breath. The amount of stuff that needed to be learned seemed astronomical – but there was also no choice really. And maybe whatever else the world did, that was a good thing, not a problem. Ways would have to be found. Experiments – tests – crazy ideas. At least there seemed no shortage of crazy ideas.

"The possibilities seem endless," he murmured.